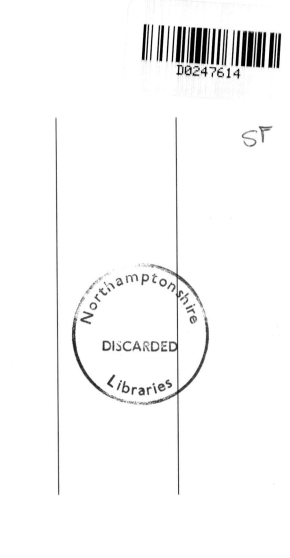

Titles in Teen Reads:

New Dawn DANIEL BLYTHE	**Raven** TOMMY DONBAVAND	**Remember Rosie** BEVERLY SANFORD
Underworld SIMON CHESHIRE	**Ward 13** TOMMY DONBAVAND	**The Wishing Doll** BEVERLY SANFORD
Dawn of the Daves TIM COLLINS	**Fair Game** ALAN DURANT	**Billy Button** CAVAN SCOTT
Joke Shop TIM COLLINS	**By My Side** ANN EVANS	**Mama Barkfingers** CAVAN SCOTT
Mr Perfect TIM COLLINS	**Nightmare** ANN EVANS	**Pest Control** CAVAN SCOTT
The Locals TIM COLLINS	**Insectoids** ROGER HURN	**The Changeling** CAVAN SCOTT
Troll TIM COLLINS	**Jigsaw Lady** TONY LEE	**The Hunted** CAVAN SCOTT
Copy Cat TOMMY DONBAVAND	**Mister Scratch** TONY LEE	**Sitting Target** JOHN TOWNSEND
Dead Scared TOMMY DONBAVAND	**Noticed** TONY LEE	**Deadly Mission** MARK WRIGHT
Just Bite TOMMY DONBAVAND	**Stalker** TONY LEE	**Ghost Bell** MARK WRIGHT
Home TOMMY DONBAVAND	**Death Road** JON MAYHEW	**The Corridor** MARK WRIGHT
Kidnap TOMMY DONBAVAND	**Snow White, Black Heart** JACQUELINE RAYNER	**World Without Words** JONNY ZUCKER

Badger Publishing Limited, Oldmedow Road, Hardwick Industrial Estate, King's Lynn PE30 4JJ
Telephone: 01438 791037

www.badgerlearning.co.uk

NEW DAWN

DANIEL BLYTHE

 Badger
LEARNING

New Dawn ISBN 978-1-78464-327-0

Text © Daniel Blythe 2015
Complete work © Badger Publishing Limited 2015

Publisher: Susan Ross
Senior Editor: Danny Pearson
Editorial Coordinator: Claire Morgan
Copyeditor: Cheryl Lanyon
Designer: Bigtop Design Ltd
Printed by Bell and Bain Ltd, Glasgow

2 4 6 8 10 9 7 5 3 1

CHAPTER 1

EDEN

Eden Boone kicked the front door so hard it slammed into the wall, taking a chunk out of the plaster. She threw her school bag down on the floor of the hall and sat heavily on the stairs.

"I'm not going back to that vile place, Dad!" she shouted.

Her voice echoed up two flights of stairs in the old Victorian terrace, and there was no reply. Eden scowled, swung round on the banister and yelled up the stairs again.

"Dad! Did you hear me?"

Only then did Eden notice the note under the fruit bowl, written in blue ink. She picked it up, peered at it.

WORKING LATE AT THE LAB. ALL-NIGHTER. ONTO SOMETHING BIG. TEA IN MICROWAVE. SEE YOU TOMORROW. LOVE DAD XX

Eden sighed, put the letter down. "Not even a text," she said out loud.

It was normal to get this kind of note from her father. He was a Professor of Physics at the University, and always busy. She had hoped tonight would be different, though. He had promised her a film and curry night, just the two of them. These evenings were important, all the more so now Mum had gone.

Also, after Eden's rubbish day, she'd been hoping to do twenty minutes of moaning in the kitchen. Stuff about not having the right shorts for stupid hockey, and Miss Bancroft picking on her again.

About what cows Courtney and Katie were being, and about how disgusting the lunch had been today. Basically, what a waste of time school was.

She stomped into the kitchen, checked out the plastic dish in the microwave. She wrinkled her nose at the lemony aroma. Thai green curry with pilau rice. Could be worse, she thought.

She flicked the TV on, watching BBC News 24 half-heartedly.

"– growing crisis in the Middle East," said the newsreader's voice, over pictures of tanks rolling along a desert road. *"The UN Emergency Council is still in session, uncertain as to how to deal with this turn of events. The President has said that in twenty-four hours, the Western world could face the horror of nuclear blackmail – unless the Geneva Conference produces the desired result."*

That didn't sound good, thought Eden. Mind

you, it was always the same, wasn't it? Someone was always fighting someone, somewhere. It usually all got sorted out.

As she closed the microwave door, she saw the two dark-suited men reflected in it. She turned around and screamed.

Eden grabbed for the kitchen knife and held it out in front of her, trying not to tremble as her heart thudded.

"What the hell?" she snapped. "Who are you? What do you want?"

The two men were seated calmly at the kitchen table. They were both bald, dressed in crisp, dark suits and mirror-shades. One was tall and thin, the other short and burly.

"Eden Boone?" said the taller man. His voice was cold, harsh.

She swung the knife round, narrowing her eyes. "Who wants to know? What the hell are you doing in my house, weirdos?"

The men gave a slow smile, together, and both flipped ID cards at her. "Special Services, Miss Boone," said the shorter man. "We need you to come with us."

She folded her arms, planted her feet firmly on the kitchen floor. "Says who?"

They stood up, and the tall man spoke again. "Your father," he replied.

Eden felt her body tingle, and unfolded her arms, her heart beating faster. "And?" she said. "Did he… say anything?"

The two men looked at one another. The taller man spoke.

"*Avocado,*" he said.

*

Thirty minutes later, after a silent drive into

the countryside during which both the men refused to answer questions, Eden was led across some scrubby wasteland towards a single, lonely warehouse.

The tall man punched a keypad on the side to open a door and they walked into its vast, cold emptiness. Eden heard their footsteps echoing on the cold stone. She could smell rust and decay.

Eden was seething with anger. But she knew her dad was in trouble and needed her because the two special agents – or whatever they were – had done something unexpected.

They had used the code word.

The word Eden and her father, Darius, had once agreed would be their special word. To show that whoever had come with a message was telling the truth.

Avocado.

They entered a lift which began to drop at a frightening rate. Just ten seconds later, the lift opened and Eden gasped.

The room was the size of a football stadium, smelling of hot metal and full of bustling activity. Beeping its horn, a fork-lift truck sped past her, carrying crates of equipment. White-coated scientists stood at a curved bank of controls, and behind them a flat wall of screens flickered with numbers. The space was filled with the babble of voices, the tap of keyboards and the click and whirr of equipment.

Eden craned her neck to look around her, amazed that somewhere like this could exist below ground, unseen.

"What the hell is this place?" Eden said aloud. She looked around for the dark-suited men, but they had gone.

"Well, you wanted to see where I worked," said a voice behind her.

Eden's eyes opened wide in delight. "Dad!"

Professor Darius Boone's bearded face broke into a toothy smile as he opened his arms to hug his daughter.

She pulled back from him, staring at him and then looking around the giant warehouse again. "But I thought you worked in a lab at the University? I'm confused."

"Well…" Professor Boone put his hands in the pockets of his white coat and nodded, "it is a lab of sorts. And it's not far from the University…" He tapped the side of his nose. "Eden, my friends the Agents brought you here because there's something you need to see. Come on."

He took his daughter's arm and led her up onto one of the metal walkways which ran around the vast space.

Holding a small remote-control, Professor Boone operated the giant bank of screens.

A square image got bigger and bigger until Eden could see it showed a beautiful, green meadow. The picture scrolled to the right and she saw jagged white cliffs, sapphire-blue seas and white spray. It all looked unreal.

"What's that?" she asked. "*Where* is it?"

"That," said Professor Boone, "is Earth. It's Earth – as it no longer is, but should be. Before humanity came along and spoiled it all. Before oil-fields, and before coal-mines, and before the ice-caps started to melt."

"What… actual pictures of it?" She did not believe him.

"No. It's a mock-up. CGI. But it's a clever 3-D model. Every pixel is based on energy readings we've had through the time hole we call the Gateway." When he turned back towards her, he had a gleam in his brown eyes, something she had not seen before. It frightened her. "This has been my passion, Eden. Why do you think I gave you that name? The Garden of Eden… a paradise we can have here on Earth."

Eden pulled a face. "Dad, you don't believe all that religious stuff!"

"Not religious, Eden." He tutted, wagged a finger. "Nothing supernatural. It's real. A parallel Earth, like our own but without the footprints of the human race. This project has been tracking it for twenty years."

"He's right, you know," said a smooth voice. A blonde, sharp-suited woman came over and shook Eden's hand. "Hello, Eden. Annie Moston. Government envoy."

Eden shook the woman's hand warily. She wasn't sure she liked her narrow face and sharp green eyes. "So you're in charge?"

Annie Moston beamed. "It's a partnership between the government and two universities."

Her face suddenly became serious. "Eden, what you and your team are about to do will literally save the world. I want you to know how very, very grateful we are."

Eden looked from her dad to Annie Moston and back again, wondering if she was going mad now, or if this was all a joke. "Save the world?" she snorted. "I think you've got the wrong girl. I can't even win on Call of Duty."

Annie Moston gave her a cold, knowing smile. "Eden," she said, "you're about to become a pioneer. One of the most important people in history. You, and three chosen… friends, are going to travel through the Gateway to the parallel world – and find out what's happened to our survey team."

Eden looked from Annie to her dad, and grinned. "This is a joke, right?" she said. "Why me?"

She thought her father's eyes looked sad, worried for a moment. Then he looked over at Annie Moston.

The woman gave a smug smile. "Preparations begin immediately," she said. "Briefing in one hour."

CHAPTER 2

THE GATEWAY

Eden didn't like the look of the three people Annie Moston had described as her 'team'.

They stood beside her in a row, lined up in Annie Moston's stark, white briefing room. Eden gave them a nervous glance.

Zach Chaney was the tallest, a boy with unruly dark hair, gleaming white teeth and sharp cheekbones. She'd have called him fit, but he also looked untrustworthy, sly. Beside him was Talia Bethany, a wiry, dark-haired girl with sharp eyes and a jittery, restless air. And then there was Kane Gordon, a boy with a blond crew-cut and tattoos, and a gold tooth – Eden thought he looked angry, resentful.

It was just starting to dawn on Eden that this wasn't a game – they actually meant it. Quantum Physics. Parallel universes. She had never really listened when her dad used to talk about it.

Annie Moston stood in front of a touch-screen which filled the whole of one wall.

"I don't know if you've noticed," she said, "but the world is in crisis. You know about this conference in Geneva right now?"

Eden nodded. She'd only just seen it on the news an hour or two ago. But at least she was telling the truth.

"It's our last, best hope for peace," said Annie Moston grimly. "If it doesn't succeed, we could be facing a war in Europe and America. A war which – let's not be all fluffy and nice about this – would mean the end of the world as we know it.

We're talking millions upon millions dead."

Eden shrugged. "So sort it out! That's what you people do, isn't it?"

Annie Moston held up a hand. "We are sorting it out. But just in case we can't – Professor Boone has a plan."

With a sweep of her hand, she made a moving picture appear – lush green forests, snowy peaks in the bright sun. It made Eden think of Switzerland, or Canada. "New Earth," said Annie Moston. "The new hope for the human race. At least – we thought so."

Kane grinned and folded his arms. "You messed it up," he said, nodding.

Annie Moston glared at him. "Not exactly."

"Yeah, but you did," said Talia. "You lost them people and now you wanna get them back. And you think we're gonna do your dirty work."

Eden, shaking with anticipation, looked at each of her companions in turn. "Is that true? Is that what we're doing?"

Annie Moston sighed, flicked the screen again. "This isn't the number 12 bus we're talking about," she said. "This is important stuff. The Holy Grail of generations of physicists. Professor Boone's team has been working on this problem for years."

The four teenagers looked at each other, and Eden noticed they were now all more interested – apart from Zach, who just stood with a smug smile and his arms folded.

Annie Moston outlined the problem in a matter-of-fact way, like a teacher. The project had been up and running for twenty years. A joint team from Oxford and Cambridge Universities had made the discovery of the century, which the government had ordered them to keep secret – what Annie called a 'cat-flap' into a parallel world. Ever since, they had worked on the portal, controlling it, making it more stable.

"Widening the cat-flap," said Eden, and everyone looked at her. She felt herself blush. "Sorry. Carry on."

Annie Moston smiled sweetly. It was quite chilling, and made Eden shudder.

She carried on. A team of scientists, led by a man called Dr Luke Mathias, had passed through the portal, with the aim of scouting out the land, making first readings and then returning within the day.

But the team had completely disappeared.

Without trace.

Annie Moston brought up a photo of Dr Mathias. He was about her dad's age, with a thin face, sharp blue eyes and high cheekbones. Eden thought he looked intelligent, kind.

"They didn't come back through at the correct pick-up time," Annie Moston explained. "Contact's been lost. We haven't had anything for five days. And that, dear things, is where you come in."

"Why us?" said Talia sulkily. Eden was glad she had asked. "I mean, there ain't nothing special about any of us, right? We ain't scientists."

"Exactly," said Annie Moston with a big, red-painted smile, and spread her hands. "We can't afford to lose more scientists. You, on the other hand, are quick to learn, young, strong – and expendable. And with a lot to lose if you don't do as you're told."

Talia scowled. "What does that mean?"

Zach spoke for the first time, his voice smooth and sneering. "What she means is," he said, "we're nobody. Right?" He looked round at the others. "This government's got it in for people like us. People who don't fit in. People who don't do as they're told. People they've spotted as trouble."

Annie Moston's smile did not waver. "I wouldn't put it quite like that."

"No," said Zach. "I bet you wouldn't."

Eden was deciding she really quite liked Zach.

"The fact is," said Annie Moston, "that we have to be careful. And that's why we've got you," she added, nodding at Eden.

Eden felt herself turn cold. "Me?" she said, her voice quiet and thin.

"Yes, you. You, my dear, are *insurance*."

Eden didn't quite understand what she meant.

*

They stood on a raised white ramp, in front of a giant metal ring about ten metres across. It glowed with white light. Cables trailed off from it on all sides, leading to instrument-banks operated by scientists.

Eden knew the metal Gateway led to something called the 'anomaly'. She didn't try to understand, but she knew it was a sort of hole in time and space. A rip in the fabric.

Her father had told her that people would be surprised just how many of them appeared. It was just that, most of the time, people didn't recognise them. They might see a flash of something weird out of the corner of their eye, or see a ghost in Victorian dress, or someone might disappear without explanation. His theory – backed up by years of evidence – was that these anomalies were the cause.

Only this time, they'd caught one.

It was, Professor Boone said, like "trapping lightning in a box" – almost impossible. But they had done it. And the anomaly – like a captured animal – was wriggling, squealing, angry in its 'box', which was a contained energy field. When the moment came, they would only have seconds to pass through it into the alternate dimension.

The foursome lined up. They had all been kitted out in one-piece suits made of some tough, flexible material.

On their wrists they had devices like digital watches, all reading 01:00:00. They were set to count down from one hour when they entered the anomaly. Annie Moston had said – very sternly – that they were not to lose these, as the watches had built-in trackers which were the team's only link with home. They had also been told that the entry point could only be kept open for short periods. They would be given an hour, after which they had to be back in the same place to return home – or they would miss their chance. "Think of it as like catching a train," Annie Moston had said, with her cold and creepy smile again.

Eden had never felt so frightened. She looked up at Zach. "I can't quite believe we're doing this," she said.

He looked down at her, and gave her a cheeky smile. "Hey, I'm totally up for it. It's better than the other life I could have."

She was puzzled. "What do you mean?"

"I set fire to my school in the Austerity Riots," he said with a shrug. "Not much of a future for me."

Eden was shocked. "And her?" she said, nodding towards Talia.

"Gang girl. Done for knife crime, joyriding." He grinned over at Kane, who was standing silently, arms folded, on the other side of the ramp. "And him? Nasty piece of work. Bullying, drugs, you name it."

It suddenly dawned on Eden why the others were doing this. "You're all going to get off. A free pardon."

"Got it in one, daddy's-girl." Zach gave that annoying, smug smile again. "But you – you're just here for insurance like the lady said."

"What did she mean?" Eden scowled. "I didn't understand."

"Your dad." Zach nodded over to where Professor Boone was bent over a computer screen with Annie Moston, deep in concentration. "You don't think he actually likes that Moston bitch, do you? He doesn't really want his research used by the government. Not yet. He wants to do years more tests."

It suddenly dawned on Eden. "But if I'm going…"

Zach thumped her on the shoulder. "You've got it, babe. Annie Moston and the government get to keep your dad in line. As long as you're on the team, she knows your dad will do his best work. He has to!"

"Places, please!" Annie Moston called out.

"Then I'll just refuse to go!" cried Eden.

"Seriously, babe." scoffed Zach. "What do you think will happen to your dad then? Scientists can be replaced!"

The Gateway was starting to pulse with white-hot energy. In the circle of steel, Eden watched the air take on a strange, fluid quality. She could taste something odd, too, like metal. There wasn't much time if she was going to back out.

"Fine" she said, gritting her teeth. "I'm doing this for my dad. But if you call me *babe* again, I'm going to have to – "

The Gateway flared with light, dazzling her.

"Go!" snapped Annie Moston. "Go now!"

The light washed over them, and then Eden's world faded into nothingness as a terrible darkness fell in her brain.

CHAPTER 3

THE DESOLATION

Eden was slammed to the ground. Her body felt both freezing cold and burning hot at the same time.

" – kill you," she heard herself say.

She realised that they'd passed through in less than the blink of an eye. Less than the time it took her to finish that threat to Zach. She had not even had to step forwards.

She sat up slowly.

She noticed a gleam of red on her wrist, and realised that her watch had started counting down – it read 00:59:30.

The pain faded. Some instinct made her scramble to her feet, her movements smooth and quick in the body-suit.

A dark figure loomed over her and she kicked, catching it in the stomach. It fell with a satisfying "oof".

It was Kane. Lying on the scorched ground beside her, clutching his stomach. He glared at her, his face screwed up in pain.

"Sorry, sorry!" She hauled him to his feet and he turned and spat on the ground.

"Jumpy already?" he snarled.

But Eden did not really take in what he said. She was looking around her.

"Kane," she said, "where the hell are we?"

The sun was low in the sky, red and swollen like a boil. They stood in what had once been a city. On the horizon, battered tower-blocks stood against the crimson sky filled with evil clouds. In the blackened plaza where they stood, they could see the broken, scorched remains of shop-fronts, glass windows twisted into odd shapes.

In front of her, Eden saw a great snake of metal which she suddenly realised, with a start, had once been a tram. It was rusted, molten, fused to its rails. Beyond that stood the remains of a cathedral, its stone charred black. Its roof and walls had caved in as if punched by a giant fist.

All around them was an eerie, unnatural stillness. No birdsong, no traffic, no sounds of any kind apart from a dim, distant howling. Like the planet moaning in pain.

She saw two shadows fall across the ground and realised that Zach and Talia had joined them.

"This isn't right," Zach muttered. He crouched, picking up a handful of crumbling tarmac.

"What is this? Wrong place?"

Eden was aware that her watch had already counted down several minutes, and that every second counted. If they weren't back in exactly the same spot at the end of the countdown, they would miss the pick-up, just like the missing survey team…

Just here for 'insurance', am I? she thought. The idea made her burn with anger. *I'll show them.*

Eden reacted in the best way she knew how. She took charge.

"Zach, you come with me. Talia, Kane…" she cast her eyes around, "start with that ruined cathedral. Any clues as to what happened here. We need to report back on everything."

00:54:22

Zach and Eden made their way through the shell of a shop. They climbed a stack of rubble and twisted girders piled like a small mountain.

Eden scrambled to the top, from where she had a better view of the ruins.

"Oh, God," she whispered softly.

"So, what are we thinking?" said Zach beside her. He sounded almost amused. "Nuclear bomb? Meteor?"

"Could have been anything," Eden reasoned.

There was a sick, plummeting feeling in her stomach. What had gone wrong? All the readings her dad's team had been getting were computer-generated. The visuals Annie Moston had shown them were CGI, they knew that. But she had expected them to be accurate. This wasteland… this was just *insane*.

"What a sad, terrible place," she murmured.

"Sheffield," said Zach suddenly.

"No, here, you idiot."

Zach nodded across the rubble-strewn square. "I don't know how, but this is – or was – Sheffield," he said. "Look."

Eden followed where he was pointing. On the left of the square, she made out the remains of a square building with glass swing-doors. The silver, boxy top of the building was stencilled with giant letters – CRUCIBLE.

Eden shook her head. "What does it mean?"

"Never watch the snooker, babe?" Zach said, with a superior smile. He nodded to the building. "The Crucible Theatre. Trust me – this was Sheffield."

Eden had no idea why the portal should have dumped them here – in this twisted, shattered version of their world. She felt deeply, angrily sad for her father and all his research. Had it been for nothing? Was this some terrible, cruel trick being played on them by Time, by Fate, by the dimensions?

Eden knew one thing, though. This place felt bad, cruel and evil. It had a vile, burnt, rotting stench. She knew she didn't feel safe here.

"Just a minute." Zach was scanning the horizon, over by the burnt tower-blocks.

Eden tensed. "What is it?"

He shook his head. "Nah. Thought I saw something, but…"

"What?"

"A flash, like a car or something moving." He shuddered. "In this light, anything's possible."

00:51:19

Talia and Kane re-joined them in the plaza. The remains of buildings loomed above them all like giant, twisted sculptures. Still the unearthly howling continued in the background, making Eden shudder.

"OK," she said. "Find anything?"

Kane shook his head, spitting onto the scorched tarmac.

"It looks like there was a war," said Talia, her face grim and pale. "There's bones and everything. Bullet-holes and stuff."

"Yeah," Kane looked nervously around him. "So there might be crazy weirdos waiting to shoot us as well. Fantastic."

"Shut up, all of you!" It was Zach, holding up a hand, and his voice was so urgent and harsh that they all stopped straight away and listened.

There was a noise. A whining, like an engine. It echoed through the deserted city, bouncing off the shells of the buildings.

The four of them looked at each other for a second.

And now Eden realised that they were waiting for her to tell them what to do.

"Take cover," she said, nodding towards the rusted shell of the department store. "Over there."

00:45:49

They hurried inside the building, crouching down.

It was open to the sky, covered in dust and debris, and twisted plants sprouted in the remains of the escalators and displays.

The vehicle appeared in the plaza and came to a screeching halt. It was a white van covered with graffiti, including a red skull-and-crossbones.

Two people got out and started walking about, like they owned the place. Eden thought they were about her age, but they were so weather-beaten that it was hard to tell. The boy had blue dreadlocks and was dressed in a biker-jacket and combat trousers. The girl had red hair, shaven close to the skull, and wore a silver jacket over a bikini top, with fake-leather leggings and red boots. Mirrored sunglasses covered her eyes.

It chilled Eden's blood to see that they were both armed – the boy with a spear, the girl with a crossbow.

Eden held up a hand. She crawled closer to the shattered doors to try and hear. She hid behind the battered remains of a shop-dummy.

"Here's where the cams picked the trace up," the girl was saying.

Eden risked peeking around the dummy. She saw, to her surprise, that the girl was looking at some kind of hand-held device – like a mobile phone, but chunkier.

"Yeah, well," said the boy, "looks like there's nowt here. Wasting time, Jana. Let's get back."

"I dunno, Arlo." The girl, Jana, cast her gaze around. "They're not usually wrong."

CRASH!

Eden jumped, looking around in horror, her heart thumping. Talia held her hands up, her eyes wide. She had knocked over a table and sent a pile of dried-up cosmetics flying.

The boy and girl outside looked at each other. The girl loaded her crossbow and the boy raised his spear.

Zach moved quickly. "Talia," he said, and the girl seemed to know in a second what he was doing. They both moved out of hiding.

"What are you doing?" Eden hissed.

"Follow us, babe, when they take us," Zach hissed. "I don't care how. Just do it."

"What?"

"We're gonna let ourselves get caught."

"Zach, no!"

"They know someone's here. If we don't do this, they'll find us all, and there'll be nobody back at the pick-up point in time."

Eden glanced at her watch.

00:36:12

She needed to make a decision. She looked at Talia. She realised that, for all her bravado, the gang-girl was shaking now, trying to hold back her tears.

Eden had assumed she was the same age as her, maybe fourteen or fifteen. Now, she realised Talia was probably only twelve years old.

Zach looked over to Eden.

She nodded.

Zach and Talia, hands held high, strode out into the windswept plaza. Into their destiny.

Eden glanced at Kane. He didn't look back at

her. He just turned away, as if he didn't care.

Outside, she saw Zach punched in the stomach and drop to the ground. She felt the pain as if it was her own. Then she saw the girl smack Talia's cheek, and saw Talia sprawling on the ground.

Eden winced, gritted her teeth. Her eyes stung with tears.

And then she saw them being bundled into the back of the van, and watched it drive away at speed into the distance.

CHAPTER 4

THE REVELATION

00:34:04

"That's it, then," said Kane coldly. "Never gonna find them."

"You think?" Eden answered. She already had a plan forming in her mind. "Come with me."

"What? Where?"

Eden had reached the foot of the overgrown escalator. She pointed upwards. "Need to get the lie of the land," she said. "Come on."

00:31:11

They stood on the blackened roof of the shop, looking out at the ruined city.

"Where the hell would they have gone?" Kane snarled. "What we gonna do, search the whole city?"

"No," said Eden. "Use it." She tapped him on the head. "They'd want to be near food, water, supplies. They've got to be close enough to get here after picking us up on whatever tracking system they've got."

She could clearly see the city set out in front of her as if on a board game. Rusted gasometers, crumbling cinemas, broken tower-blocks. The city was dead beneath a grey sky, and the evening sun was weak, pale. Clouds squatted on the towers and hills, looking uglier and blacker than any she had ever seen. And that weird, alien howl of abandonment echoed across the valleys.

"If there were a lot of people, we'd see them," Eden reasoned. "We'd hear them. Well, I've not heard anything. Not even any dogs or rats."

She looked beyond the shattered, burnt rooftops to the chunky towers on the ridge beyond.

The shape of the dark clouds above them had changed.

And she saw that they weren't clouds.

That was smoke.

Eden allowed herself a slow, cautious smile. "I think I know where they went," she said.

00:23:02

"Do you actually know what you're doing?" Kane snarled.

He was holding on to the battered roof of the car as they pounded through the ruins of Sheffield.

Eden had driven a car once before, on a track on Uncle Rory's farm. She didn't remember much about it, but at least there was nothing else on the road to get in the way. It hadn't been hard to find one here – or a rusting hulk of one – and Eden was amazed to find it still had petrol in the tank.

"Stop distracting me," she said. And then, as they rounded the corner, she heard herself say, "Oh, hell. Here we go."

The road up to the tower-blocks was barricaded with petrol cans and crates. The barrier was draped with banners and painted with the red skull-and-crossbones sign.

Eden took her foot off the accelerator.

They got out of the car as five or six young people approached them, dressed in a wild mixture of fashions, faces smeared with paint. Their unwashed hair was braided into strange shapes. The leader, a tall, black girl with a nose-ring, aimed a crossbow at Eden's heart.

"Yeah, when Zach said follow them," Kane drawled, "I think he kind of meant secretly. Without being caught. Yeah?"

"Shut up, Kane," she hissed. "I know what I'm doing."

"You'd better."

"I've… come to see Arlo," announced Eden. Her mouth was dry and she was shaking, but she spread her arms wide to show she was unarmed. "Please. We don't mean you any harm."

"Nobody just comes to see Arlo," said the girl. She sounded Scottish, Eden thought. "Where you from?"

"You'd never believe me."

"Try me."

Eden decided the truth was not a good idea. "France," she said. "We've just arrived. We…

well, we kind of missed when it all… kicked off."

The girl stared at Eden blankly.

"OK. Look, does it matter? We're in this city by accident. We don't want to take anything of yours. We're just looking for some people who came here. A guy called Dr Luke Mathias and his assistant."

The Scottish girl put a hand to her ear. Only now did Eden see that she was wearing a radio earpiece, receiving orders.

The girl nodded, and suddenly Eden and Kane were surrounded by spears and crossbows.

"Move it," said the girl.

00:19:57

They were dragged roughly by their arms, their ragged captors not caring if they hurt them.

The tower-blocks formed a barrier above the city, like the ruined walls of an arena. Beyond it was a space which Eden guessed had once been green. The stench of rubbish and decay made her retch. A big bonfire burned, crackling and sparkling, sending rancid black smoke up into the sky – the clouds Eden had seen from the ruined shop.

There were more of them there. They wore a mixture of streetwear, army gear and tribal markings. She spotted Arlo straight away from his blue dreadlocks. Jana, the girl with the shaved head and mirror-shades, was there too.

And there, a sight which sickened and chilled her: Zach and Talia, hands bound to a horizontal pole, guarded by two boys with spears and crossbows. Zach had a bruise beneath his eye, and Talia's lip was bleeding.

Arlo came forwards, sharpening a knife on a stone. "So," he said coldly, "come to fetch your mates back?" He gave her a gap-toothed, yellow grin. "Or maybe come to watch them die?"

Eden and Kane looked at each other. "We don't want any trouble," Eden said, trying to sound brave. "Let us have Zach and Talia back, and we'll be on our way."

The arena rang to the sound of mocking laughter.

"Look," Eden said, "we came here searching for someone. But we're in the wrong place. We need to go back and try again. So please, just let us go."

She was full of questions. What had happened here, and how long ago? How did this ragged bunch survive? What did they eat? They probably looted warehouses and factories, she thought, looking around at the piles of tins and other rubbish. But that wouldn't last forever.

These people weren't making a society. They were on the edge of extinction.

Eden realised, with a chill of horror, that these were the last days of the human race.

"I know who you're looking for," said Arlo. "You said his name to Izzy back there. Dr Mathias. Dr Luke Mathias."

"How do you— ?"

Jana had joined them at Arlo's side. She nodded sadly. "Luke Mathias, and his assistant Liese, were here," she said. "Around the time this happened." She gestured out at the city.

Kane stepped forwards. "Hang on. That don't make sense."

"Oh, yeah. It does. You want to know?" she said. She took off her sunglasses, came right up to Eden.

Eden found herself looking into sharp, bright blue eyes.

They reminded her of something. A second later, she remembered. That picture of Dr Mathias which Annie Moston had shown them, back in the briefing room.

"They were my parents," said Jana.

00:17:29

For a second, Eden could not make sense of this.

"You expected us not to believe you," Arlo said with a cruel smile. "About who you are, and where you've come from. But that's the thing. We believe you."

Eden was starting to realise this herself.

"And that's gonna be your problem," Arlo added.

"Always wondered if the Rift would open again," said Arlo. "Knew it was just a matter of time till we got a way out of his hell-hole."

"Where are they?" Eden asked, her voice croaking with emotion. "Dr Mathias and Liese?"

Jana shrugged. "Dunno." She unfurled a crumpled photograph from her pocket and showed it to Eden. It was battered and creased, but it unmistakably showed Dr Mathias with his bright-eyed, high-cheekboned face, and a young, blonde-haired woman. "They're dead now. There were… a lot of bad things happening in the old times."

The old times. The girl's use of the phrase suddenly made Eden realise. Dr Mathias and his team had been here. They had been unable to return, so had tried to make some kind of life for themselves in this place.

Somehow, the portal had taken Eden's team through not just into the 'wrong' parallel world, but the 'wrong' time too.

Years had passed here. How many years?

"How old are you?" Eden asked Jana.

Jana shrugged. "Dunno. Seasons are all wrong, now." She nodded up at the ugly, boiling red sun.

Oh, Dad, I'm so sorry, Eden was thinking. The survey team had arrived in the wrong universe –

and now the rescue team had done the same, but too late to help.

"Enough of this," said Arlo, and roughly shoved Jana aside. The girl stared at him with murderous eyes. "We need to move out."

Eden was still unable to speak, but Kane stepped forwards, jabbing Arlo in the chest. "We ain't going nowhere," he said, "until— "

Arlo moved so fast it made Eden gasp. He slashed with the knife, slicing Kane's cheek so that the boy fell with a yelp, blood spattering on the ground. Kane had his hand to his face, but Eden could see it was a nasty cut – not fatal, but enough to be painful.

"Next time," said Arlo coldly, "it goes deeper." He started issuing orders. "Izzy, cut those two down and bring them. Jana – get the van."

"Where are we going?" Eden asked, looking up from pressing her sleeve into Kane's bloodied face.

Arlo gave her a broken, gap-toothed grin. "On a little journey. Because you guys are what we've been looking for all this time. How long you got?" He nodded at the watch on Eden's wrist.

She glanced at the display. **00:14:55**.

"Just under a quarter of an hour."

"Nice one," said Arlo. "*Move it.* Into the van."

As she was bundled roughly into the back of the van with the others, Eden had the horrible feeling she knew what Arlo wanted.

And now she knew she had to stop him.

CHAPTER 5

DEADLINE

00:08:13

"What happened here?" Eden asked.

They were in near-darkness in the back of the van, as it jolted and bumped along. Jana and Izzy were guarding the four of them, Jana pointing her crossbow almost lazily at the bruised, subdued Zach.

"It all went wrong," said Jana quietly. "Started in the Middle East when they got nukes. Some kind of peace conference failed. In Geneva."

Eden gasped. She was talking about the conference that was happening right now, back at home! They hadn't travelled to a parallel universe at all. They had time-travelled to the future – or at least a possible future.

Back home, they were at the tipping-point. The moment which could plunge their world into fire and darkness, and turn it into this one.

"What happened?"

Jana shrugged. "A war. First one city bombed, then another. London's a crater, Birmingham's still radioactive. Nobody goes down there any more."

"And the rest of the world?"

"Most of Europe's just wasteland. But they say bits of Africa are still doing all right, and America."

"How do you survive?" Eden whispered.

Jana's nostrils flared. "We do what we can. Some stuff still grows. You'd be surprised. And there's animals. You soon learn how to kill. How to live."

"And if you don't?" Zach asked.

Jana looked over at Izzy, who made a hissing noise and slid her finger across her throat.

Eden shuddered.

"Loads died." Jana's voice was matter-of-fact. "Reckon there's, like, ten thousand people left in England."

Eden didn't dwell on that. "You know… you don't have to do as he says," she told Jana. She nodded towards the front of the van, where Arlo sat.

"Someone has to be leader. We decided that a long time ago."

"What's in it for you?"

"Shut up," Jana retorted. But Eden sensed a small spark there. Something. If only she could…

The van jolted to a halt. Arlo cut the engine.

The doors were flung open and Eden saw, in the cold light of the setting sun, that they were back in the plaza where they had arrived.

She could see, now it was darker, the orange specks of fires burning up on hills in different parts of the city. Other survivors, she thought. She wondered if they were as tough as this bunch.

"Get out." Izzy gestured with her crossbow and they clambered out of the van.

As Zach got down, his hands still tied, his eyes met Eden's and she nodded.

Zach span his entire body round, spinning on one heel.

With his hands balled together into a double fist, he smacked Izzy, sending her sprawling on the ground. Kane reacted quickly too, stamping on Izzy's leg and making her scream in pain.

In the same moment, Eden charged into Jana, slamming her into the side of the van. The crossbow came free from Jana's hand, skittering across the ground. Talia snatched it up, and pointed it straight at Arlo as he lunged towards them.

"Don't try it," Talia snapped.

Eden glanced at her watch. **00:04:17**. Four minutes, seventeen seconds until the nightmare ended.

"I hope they're on time for the pick-up," she muttered.

And then, she felt the world spinning and she crashed to the ground, her head smacking on the tarmac with intense, angry pain. She was dimly aware that someone – Izzy – had grabbed her ankle, pulled her down.

She rolled over.

She tried to pull herself up, but a boot slammed into her chest, knocking the breath from her.

It was Izzy. She had her crossbow pointed at Eden's head.

"Drop it, bitch," said Izzy to Talia. "Unless you want your friend dead."

Eden, her body cold with fear, glanced over towards Zach and Kane. They looked helpless.

Talia slumped, defeated.

In a second, Jana had grabbed a spear and had them covered.

"Now, then," said Arlo, swaggering over to Eden and taking her wrist in his rough hand. He leered at her, his yellowing teeth like tombstones. The blue dreads made him look like some ancient warrior claiming his prize. "I need this. Don't I?" He nodded down at the watch. "So you can either give it to me, or…" He drew a knife from his belt and held it to Eden's wrist. "I can just take it."

"Don't be stupid," Zach told him. "You don't know what you're doing."

"Oh, I do, mate. This world's going to hell. Nowt left here worth living for, right? It'll all be over here in a year. But you… you've come from a better place." He nodded to Eden. "You, girly, you're my way out."

"You can't do that." Eden heard the panic in her own voice. "You don't belong in our world. It's not for you."

The dial read **00:02:23**.

"Us too," Jana said. Eden could not read her eyes behind the mirror-shades, but she heard the uncertainty in her voice. "We go too, Arlo. That was the deal."

"Whatever," Arlo sneered, and ripped the watch from Eden's wrist, tearing the skin and drawing blood. Eden screamed, clutching her wrist, feeling the intense pain like fire on her skin. She tried to speak as salty tears washed down her face.

Zach, Kane and Talia could not move.

00:01:56

Something was happening. The plaza seemed to be vibrating with light and sound. A circle of pale fire blossomed in the air, like a demon suddenly appearing out of nowhere, dazzling them.

Jana lifted the spear.

"I'm so sorry," she said calmly.

A flash of movement, and a thud. Arlo was thrown back, a red stain blossoming on his shirt. The wound spouted dark red blood as he fell on the ground, screaming.

Izzy wavered, the crossbow lowered. Her delayed reaction was the chance they needed.

"Go," Jana said, nodding at Zach, Talia and Kane. "Go now!"

They looked at one another, held hands and jumped into the burning circle of the anomaly.

00:00:34

Eden grabbed her watch, and with trembling hands replaced it on her bleeding wrist.

"Why?" she said to Jana.

Jana was calm, cold. "Something my father did has to have some meaning," she said. "Someone's gotta have hope. This can't be all there is."

"He's not dead, is he?" Eden asked, nodding down at Arlo.

Jana's eyes were sad, but she shook her head. "He'll remember me doing that, though. Might make him think twice in future."

Eden nodded. The two girls looked at each other for a second longer, then shook hands.

Two girls from different timelines, who should never even have met.

Eden Boone braced herself, and jumped…

00:00:00

She hit the metal ramp, sliding down, battered and bruised.

As she scrambled to her feet, reality took shape around her. Behind her, the heat and the screaming whine of the Gateway faded away.

She was looking up into the astonished face of Annie Moston.

"Nice to see you," Eden said. "We've got some news for you."

Seconds later, her father was there, hugging her tightly. A short distance away, Kane, Zach and

Talia were recovering, being looked after and given water.

"We didn't find Dr Mathias's party," Eden told her father. "But I know what happened to them."

"You do?" He looked shocked.

"Yeah. Long story. You're never gonna believe us." Eden looked around at all the equipment. "You know what, Dad? What you do is great, but… I don't know if it's the way to find a new home for humanity." She shuddered. "Something about us. We always find a way to mess it up."

Annie Moston strode over, arms folded. "What are you saying?"

Eden gave a tired smile. "Maybe we all need to focus on this world, yeah? So get back to your government, Miss Moston, and get them to make sure that conference succeeds."

Annie Moston raised an eyebrow. "All right, Eden. I don't need a teenager to tell me my job.

I know what'll happen if it fails."

Eden's eyes met Zach's and she saw him give a tired grin and a nod.

"So do we," she said grimly. "We've been there."

THE END